You Don't Look Like Your Mother

To Karle—A.F.

For my beautiful grandmother, Angelina
With thanks to A.C., D.C., L.B., J.L., and M.M.—L.J.

Text copyright © 2002 by Aileen Fisher
Illustrations © 2002 by Lilith Jones

With thanks to Sarah Ruppert, Volunteers For Wildlife, Huntington, New York

For information contact:
MONDO Publishing
980 Avenue of the Americas
New York, NY 10018
Visit our web site at http://www.mondopub.com

Printed in the United States of America
02 03 04 05 06 07 HC 9 8 7 6 5 4 3 2 1
02 03 04 05 06 07 PB 9 8 7 6 5 4 3 2 1

ISBN 1-58653-856-X (hardcover)   ISBN 1-59034-061-2 (pbk.)

Designed by Marina Maurici
Production by Danny Adlerman

You Don't Look Like Your Mother

By Aileen Fisher

Illustrated by Lilith Jones

The robin perched where aspens grow
and peered into the ferns below.

4

"Whose child are you down there," she said,
"with spots of white on brownish red?"

The fawn looked up and twitched an ear.

"My mother is a tan-gray deer."

"A deer!" The robin sat up tall. "How does she know you're hers at all? With dapples big and dapples small, you don't look like your mother."

The robin stared, her head aslant. "Whose child is on that milkweed plant," she asked, "with stripes of white and black and yellow curved around his back?"

The caterpillar blinked an eye. "You ask," he said, "whose child am I? My mother is a butterfly."

"A butterfly!" the robin cried. "You're not like any I have spied. You're long and round, not thin and wide. You don't look like your mother."

Beside the pond, upon its brink, the robin
bent her head to drink.

"Whose child are you?" She blinked an eye
as someone's head and tail swam by.

"Who, me?" exclaimed the polliwog.
"My mother is a hoppy frog."

"A hoppy frog? How can that be?" the robin
cried excitedly. "You don't look like a frog to me.
You don't look like your mother."

"What yellow balls of fluff are these?" the robin chirped.

"They float with ease
like little bobbing puffs of sun
moving softly one by one."

A ball of yellow wagged its head.
"Our mother is a duck," it said.

"A duck!" the robin cried. "All white
and feather-smooth and watertight?
I really can't believe my eyes.
You don't look like your mother."

"Whose babies can these squeakers be inside
the knothole in this tree?" the robin asked.
"I cannot think whose children are so small and pink."

A squeaky voice inside the house said (squeak!)
"Our mother is a mouse."

"A mouse all gray and velvety?" the robin asked.

"How can it be she knows you're hers? It's plain to see you don't look like your mother."

Then to her nest the robin flew.

She laid five eggs of greenish blue.

She brooded them as robins do.

And then the strangest thing occurred.
Each robin egg produced a bird.

What naked, scrawny chicks—my word!
But did the robin seek a clue and want to know,
"Whose chicks are you?"

And did she ever doubt? Oh, no.
She cared for every one just so, and sang,
"You're wonderful, although...

...you don't look like your mother!"